ISBN 0-7097-0930-7

©1995 Brown Watson, England

This edition first published 1995 by Brown Watson

The Old Mill, 76 Fleckney Road
Kibworth Beauchamp
Leicester LE8 0HG

Printed in Germany

LITTLE WOMEN

By Louisa May Alcott
Retold by Maureen Spurgeon
Illustrated by George Fryer

Brown Watson

ENGLAND

One cold, snowy December day, four sisters sat by the fire, talking by the light of the oil lamp on the table. There was Margaret, the eldest, (everyone called her Meg), Josephine, known as Jo, Beth (short for Elizabeth) and Amy, the youngest. It was almost Christmastime – although, as they all agreed, it did not feel very much like Christmas. Their father was serving in the American Civil War as an Army Chaplain, and they all missed him very much.

It was soon after the clock had struck six and Beth had toasted some bread for tea, that Mrs. March came back from town. "I've got a treat for you after supper!" she said, patting the pocket in her cloak.

Their mother – the girls called her Marmee – had a letter from their father, full of cheerfulness and hope rather than the dangers of war. "When I return," he wrote, "I shall be fonder and prouder than ever of my little women." Even tomboy Jo wept as Marmee finished reading.

Christmas morning dawned cold and grey. The girls were glad to see a bright fire burning in the kitchen, where Hannah, who had lived with them since Meg was born, was getting breakfast.

They put their presents for Marmee in a basket – cologne from Amy, handkerchieves from Beth, slippers and a pair of gloves from Meg. Then Meg hid the basket under the sofa, leaving Hannah in charge of the food.

"She went to see them poor Hummels," she said when they asked where Marmee was. "Six children and a new baby with no fire, nor nothing to eat." The girls looked at each other. How could they eat their breakfast of buckwheat cakes, cream and muffins now? They packed the food and hurried through the snow to the Hummels, with Hannah bringing wood for a fire. Marmee was dressing the baby as they arrived, the other children huddled together under an old quilt.

"If this is loving our neighbour," said Meg, as the children ate and warmed themselves, "then I like it!" Later on, after Marmee had thanked the girls for their presents and the Christmas games were played, they had a surprise of their own, a table spread with ice cream, cake, fruit, sweets – and four bunches of flowers! "Mr. Laurence sent them," smiled Marmee. "Hannah told one of his servants about your breakfast party for the Hummels and he thought you should be rewarded!"

That was another surprise! They hardly ever saw Mr. Laurence, the old gentleman who lived next door. Then Meg and Jo met his grandson, Laurie, when they were invited to a New Year's Eve party given by the Gardiners, the wealthiest family in the neighbourhood. Everyone else seemed far more elegant and better dressed. But, as Meg and Jo told each other afterwards, nobody else had the treat of being driven home in Laurie's carriage!

After they had said goodnight to Laurie, Jo and Meg crept indoors. As their bedroom door creaked open, Beth and Amy cried out together,

"Tell us about the party!"

Jo had saved some sweets for the younger sisters, and they were soon quiet as mice, hearing from Meg and Jo about the music and the dancing and all the people who had been there.

The next meeting with Laurie came when he appeared at a window and called out to Jo. "I've had a bad cold! Can you come and read to me?" Jo went to ask Marmee. And when Laurie's tutor showed her in to the Laurence's house, Jo had with her a blancmange from Meg, flowers from Amy, and two kittens from Beth! "I know Beth," cried Laurie. "I often look out and see you all with your mother." Jo could see his lips trembling as he raked over the fire. "I haven't any mother, you know."

Jo felt sorry for him. "I wish you'd come over and see us," she said. "We have got to know all our neighbours, except you."

There was a portrait of his grandfather hanging in the library. "Why are we afraid of him?" she wondered aloud, looking up at the kind eyes and the firm mouth. "I like him!"

"Thank you, ma'am!" came the voice of Mr. Laurence behind her. Jo whirled around and he shook her hand. "Let's go and have tea with that grandson of mine!" Afterwards Jo persuaded Laurie to play the splendid grand piano. She wondered why Mr. Laurence didn't seem to enjoy it much.

"That may be because Laurie's mother was a musician," Marmee said when Jo mentioned it. "She was a beautiful, clever Italian lady. But Mr. Laurence's father did not want his son to marry her." Hearing all this made shy-natured Beth even more afraid of the old man, although Jo, Meg and even little Amy liked him.

"The boy neglects his music," Mr. Laurence told Marmee one day. "Wouldn't one of your girls like to practise on the piano, just to keep it in tune?"

Beth stepped forward, almost clapping her hands. The thought of practising on that splendid instrument quite took her breath away! And when Mr. Laurence rose, as if he were going, she made up her mind to speak.

"I'll come!" cried Beth, all fears forgotten. "If you're sure nobody will be disturbed . . ." She never knew Mr. Laurence often opened his study door when she was in his house to hear her play. Beth was so grateful that she decided to make Mr. Laurence some slippers and set to work at once. A few days later, she was coming back from a walk, when Amy called out to her.

"Quick, Beth! You've got a letter from Mr. Laurence! And he's sent you . . ." But Jo shut the window, leaving Beth to wonder what Amy was talking about!

At the door, her sisters took hold of Beth and led her through the house, all pointing and all talking at once.

There in the parlour was the most beautiful little piano, as lovely as the one she played in Mr. Laurence's house. In his letter to Beth, Mr. Laurence said the piano had belonged to his grand-daughter who had died.

"You'll have to go and thank him!" smiled Jo, giving Beth a nudge. And when her sisters saw Mr. Laurence walking with his back to their gate, Amy nearly fell out of the window with surprise.

Nobody, least of all Beth, could believe that she had ever been afraid of the old gentleman.

By now, Jo had seen Amy. She knew that her sister could not have heard Laurie's warning, but she said nothing. "Let her take care of herself!" she thought, still very angry. But Amy was determined to speak to Jo, and after she put her skates on she went towards her, taking a path across the smoother ice in the middle of the river. Suddenly, there was a terrible cry that made Jo's heart stop still. Amy had fallen through the broken ice, into the freezing river.

For a second, Jo could only stand, staring terror-stricken at Amy's head above the black water. What was she to do?

"Bring a rail from the fence!" cried Laurie. "Quick, quick!"

How she and Laurie got Amy out of the water and safely home, Jo never knew. The whole time Marmee was taking off her wet things and bandaging Amy's cuts and bruises, Jo kept thinking that it would have been her fault if Amy had died. "All because I wouldn't forgive her," she told herself. "If Laurie hadn't been there to help, it would have been too late." When Amy finally opened her eyes and smiled at Jo, they hugged each other close, and all was forgiven and forgotten.

"You think your temper is the worst in the world, Jo," said Marmee, kissing her wet cheek. "But mine used to be just like it." And Jo was so surprised, she forgot to cry.

After all the snow, spring-time was more than welcome. Meg was invited to stay with her friend, Sallie Moffat. When it came to a party they were giving, Sallie and her big sister, Belle, crimped and curled Meg's hair, rouged her cheeks and gave her a splendid gown to wear, with lots of jewellery. Jo sent Laurie along to see how Meg looked. "Wouldn't Jo be surprised if she saw me?" smiled Meg, in all her finery.

"Yes," said Laurie solemnly. "I think you might be right."

"Don't you like me this way?" Meg asked him.

"No," said Laurie bluntly, "I don't. I like you best as you really are, Meg."

Meg was disappointed, but then she thought about what Laurie had said. Why pretend to be somebody different to the person she really was?

In any case, the Moffats' party was soon over, and the lengthening days brought so much to do and enjoy, planting a flower garden, and going for walks and rowing trips along the river.

Even when it rained, there was always plenty for the girls to do, playing games, reading books and writing their own newspaper.

Then one Saturday morning they got up to find no fire in the kitchen, no breakfast, and no Marmee.

"Mother isn't sick," Meg told them, "only very tired. She isn't a bit like her usual self."

"We'll have to look after ourselves!" cried Jo. "What fun!"

"Housekeeping ain't no joke," announced Hannah, but nobody listened. Meg cooked breakfast for Marmee – stewed tea, a burned omelette and soggy biscuits. Jo was sure she could do much better.

"I'll get the dinner!" she told Meg, even though she knew less about cooking than her sister. "You just keep your hands nice and give orders! I am sure I will manage."

But after a week in which she used salt instead of sugar, under-cooked the potatoes, over-cooked the greens, burned the bread and made the lumpiest blancmange ever, Jo was glad that Laurie and her sisters made her laugh about it all.

"I'll sew the shirts for Father!" Meg then decided, and Amy offered to make the buttonholes, leaving Beth to study her music. Marmee and Hannah were just thinking that the girls deserved a treat, when Laurie sent a note about a picnic party he was giving for some English visitors!

"I want to have a good time," he wrote, "and I want you all to come. I'll see to the food and everything else!"

The whole thing sounded very exciting!

"Lunch, croquet . . ." Jo read aloud, "games . . . Doesn't it sound perfect?" It was a lovely day for a picnic, too, just right for rowing up-river to Longmeadow where Laurie had set up a tent. Luckily, they had their game of croquet before noon, when the sun was really hot. After lunch and some more games, John Brooke, Laurie's tutor, and Meg got talking. "You'd enjoy teaching," he told her, "with Laurie as a pupil. When he goes to college next year, I shall join the Army."

"I suppose all young men want to do that," agreed Meg. "But it's hard for the women at home."

"I have nobody to care about me," said Brooke.

"Well, we should be very sorry to have any harm come to you," Meg smiled, pleased to see that her words cheered him a little.

At sunset, the tent came down, hampers were packed, boats loaded and they all went home, singing merrily. It had been a day to remember, and in more ways than one.

All too soon the summer ended and the days grew chilly once more. Marmee began getting worried when weeks passed without hearing from Father. She was about to ask Laurie if he would call at the Post Office to see if there was any mail, when there was a ring at the bell. "One of them horrid telegraph things!" announced Hannah. Marmee took it from her, her face very pale.

"Your husband is very ill," it said. *"Come at once. Signed, S.HALE, Blank Hospital, Washington."*

For many minutes there was only the sound of sobbing in the room, as the November day darkened outside.

The girls gathered around their mother, feeling as if all the happiness they had ever known was about to go from their lives.

"The Lord keep the dear man," croaked Hannah. "Get your things ready, right away, mum!"

But the biggest problem was finding the money for Marmee's journey to Washington. Mr. Laurence offered to help, but in the end a rich, old aunt sent the fare – with a note reminding the family how she had warned Father against going into the Army and hoping they would take her advice in future! Marmee said nothing, but she bit her lip the whole time her trunk was being packed.

Then Jo rushed out of the house. When she returned, it was with twenty five dollars! "My dear!" gasped Marmee. "How did you get it?"

"I only sold what was my own!" cried Jo, taking off her bonnet. Her beautiful, long hair had been cut. "I asked at the barber's if they bought hair and what they would give for mine. It will do my brains good to feel that mop taken off!"

Nobody wanted to go to bed that night. They knew that a cold, grey dawn would surely follow.

Everything seemed very strange when they came downstairs – having breakfast so much earlier than usual, and seeing Hannah going around the kitchen in her night-cap.

The hardest part was waving goodbye to Marmee. After she'd gone, it seemed a long time before they heard from her, but the news was good. Father was getting better, and when they all wrote letters from home, it seemed to bring them closer. There was news, too, of the Hummel's baby, who was sick. Not long after Beth had been to see them, she began feeling ill herself. The Doctor said she had Scarlet Fever. "If Mrs. March can leave her husband," he added, "she should be sent for."

Soon after, Laurie brought a letter to say that Mr. March was better. That was when Jo decided she would send for her mother.

"Mother's on her way!" the girls whispered to each other. "Marmee's coming!" And as old Hannah sat and watched, suddenly Beth's breathing became easier, as if she had just fallen asleep. Never did the world seem so lovely as it did to Meg and Jo the next morning. There was a ring at the door, a cry from Hannah – and Laurie's voice.

"Girls, she's here! Your mother's come!" Seeing Marmee made Beth feel even better, although she was still weak and had to stay in bed.